The Child's World of
KINDNESS

Library of Congress Cataloging in Publication Data

Moncure, Jane Belk.
Kindness / Jane Belk Moncure
p.   cm.
Originally published: c1980.
Summary: Simple text and scenes depict such demonstrations of
kindness as giving someone else a turn on the swing, being gentle
with puppy, helping grandfather rake leaves, and buttoning the
sweater of someone who can't do it.
ISBN 1-56766-293-5 (hardcover)
1. Kindness—Juvenile literature.   [1. Kindness.]   I. Title.
BJ1533.K5M58   1996
177'.7—dc20
                            96-11865
                            CIP
                            AC

The Child's World of
KINDNESS

By Jane Moncure • Illustrated by Mechelle Ann

THE CHILD'S WORLD

What is kindness?

Kindness is when you make a card for a friend who has the chicken pox.

When your sister jumps out of the waves, all shivery wet, and you give her your towel, that's kindness.

Kindness is when you hold the umbrella mostly over the other person when you walk in the rain.

Kindness is helping your grandfather rake leaves, even when no one asks you to do it.

Kindness is being gentle when you play with your puppy, or pick up a frog, or hold a grasshopper in your hand.

Kindness is when you make a surprise birthday cake for your mom, or when you bring your dad a glass of lemonade when he is hot.

When a friend forgets his lunch box, kindness is giving him part of your sandwiches.

Kindness is when you give a friend some of your ice-cream, because she dropped her's on the ground.

Kindness is giving someone a turn to swing on your swing, or to slide down your slide, or to sit in your wagon and take a ride.

When a friend breaks your model airplane by mistake and then wants a piece of your bubble gum, and you give it to him—that's kindness.

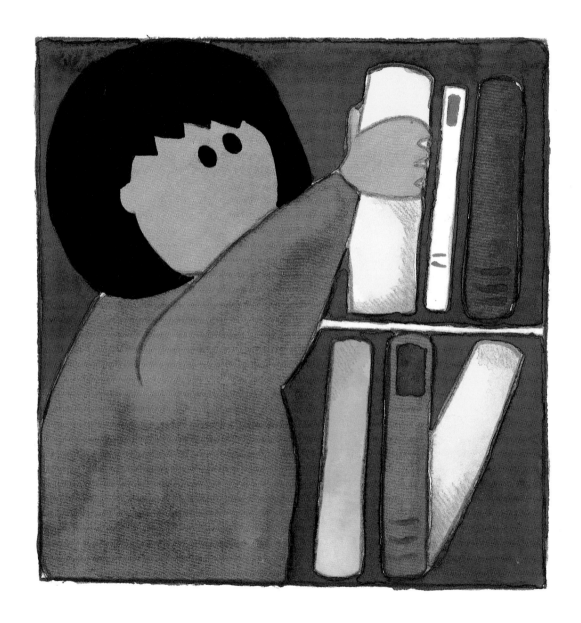

Kindness is when you help put the books back on the shelf.

Kindness brings happiness to others.

Can you think of other ways to show kindness?